THUNDER RAKER

JUSTIN RICHARDS has written many books, including Dr Who novels, the Invisible Detective series and the Time Runners series. He is also the co-author with Jack Higgins of two teenage thrillers, *Sure Fire* and *Death Run*. He lives in Warwick with his wife, two sons and a nice view of the castle. Agent Alfie is his first series for younger readers.

AGENT ALFIE
THUNDER RAKER

Justin Richards

Illustrations by Jim Hansen

HarperCollins *Children's Books*

First published in Great Britain by HarperCollins *Children's Books* 2008

HarperCollins *Children's Books* is a division of
HarperCollins*Publishers* Ltd
77-85 Fulham Palace Road, Hammersmith, London W6 8JB

The HarperCollins *Children's Books* website address is
www.harpercollinschildrensbooks.co.uk

3

ISBN-13 978-0-00-727357-7

Printed and bound in England by
Clays Ltd, St Ives plc

Mixed Sources
Product group from well-managed
forests and other controlled sources
www.fsc.org Cert no. SW-COC-1806
© 1996 Forest Stewardship Council

FSC is a non-profit international organisation established to promote the
responsible management of the world's forests. Products carrying the FSC
label are independently certified to assure consumers that they come
from forests that are managed to meet the social, economic and
ecological needs of present and future generations.

Find out more about HarperCollins and the environment at
www.harpercollins.co.uk/green

For Chris – whose dad is a writer. No, really.

Welcome to Thunder Raker Manor

An Introduction to the School
By Mr Trenchard, Head Teacher

Thunder Raker Manor is an exclusive school
for boys and girls from 8 to 18. Some of the
children come daily, some are boarders. Some
of them I remember, some of them I—— er,
what was I saying?

Anyway, all our students are here because
their parents or guardians are connected
with the Security Services. Spies and agents
are happy to send their children to Thunder
Raker Manor secure in the knowledge that
they will be safe from any possible threats.

We teach a full curriculum at Thunder
Raker, fully compliant with the National
Thingummy. And alongside the English and
Maths and History and Geography, our
students learn skills that may just come in
handy back home or in their future careers

— if they have inherited their parents'
inclinations and aptitudes.

As well as being an honorary CT (Classified
Training) Academy, Thunder Raker is
especially pleased with its latest SATS
results. We take the Special Agent Training
Standards very seriously indeed and have
achieved excellent levels in Surveillance,
Code-Breaking, and Sabotage.

And if the Security Services need a bit of
help from some youngsters for a special
mission, or if the villainous agents of that
dastardly organisation known only as the
Secret Partners for Undertaking Destruction
(S.P.U.D.) try to take over the school or
kidnap one of the teachers — rest assured,
every one of our students is ready and
prepared.

Mr Trenchard has been the Head Teacher of
Thunder Raker Manor since Mrs Muldoom's
unfortunate accident on the assault course
all those years ago. He is superbly qualified
and takes great pride in his work. When he
can remember what it is. Very good — carry
on. Um. Yes...

Mr Trenchard

**Colonel Hugh Dare-Swynne's
Class of the Week**
This week the Colonel focuses on
Class 3D, which is taught by
Miss Jones.

Miss Jones

Miss Jones says:

3D is a lovely class and works hard.
This week was especially exciting
for everyone as we had a new student
start — Alfie (surname classified).
Alfie is already settling in very
well, and even has his own cover
story — some nonsense about his
father actually being a postman.
As if!

Alfie

Alfie fits in well with the other children. He is nine years old, and he's a clever, practical boy with lots of common sense. He's brave and loyal and fun. Though I have to say he doesn't always quite understand some of the lessons or the way we do things here at Thunder Raker. But his common sense approach is a breath of fresh air and he sees the world — and our problems — in a much less cluttered and complicated way than the other children..

Jack

Next up is Jack. Jack's dad is head of the Secret Service, though of course we don't mention that. But it does explain why Jack's a bit full of himself. He is always coming up with terrific ideas and plans, though usually they are rather impractical and just too involved ever to work.

Harry's dad has infiltrated SPUD and
sends him strange, coded text messages
and letters written in invisible ink.
Sometimes the children have to go and
rescue or help him, which cuts into the
school day. Harry isn't the brightest of
the bunch by a long way, but his
questions often throw up problems with
Jack's ideas. He is brave and loyal and
willing and likes doing PE — on the
school assault course.

Sam

Sam's mum works in Whitehall for
Hush Hush, designing equipment for
agents and spies. Sam uses a
motorised wheelchair — which looks
ordinary but has amazing gadgets
built into it. Sam's mum made him
his wheelchair because the NHS
one didn't have a very good
anti-missile protection system.
And one of the wheels was wonky.

Chloe

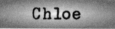

Moving on to the girls, Chloe is the
daughter of a renowned spy (and
doesn't she know it). If you thought
Jack was a bit full of himself, he's
got nothing on Chloe. She just has to
be the centre of attention, wearing
the latest fashion — and spying —
accessories. At home she's got her
telly wired up with a Playstation 3,
a Wii, and the very latest
omni-processing decryptortron.
Unfortunately Alfie isn't terribly
impressed by all this, so he and Chloe
haven't really hit it off.

Alice

Alice's dad is a double agent (but
it's a bit unclear which side
he's actually on). You never know
where you are with Alice — she
says one thing then does another.
Her moods are volatile and she's
got a temper like a tank-buster
missile when it goes off.

Beth

Beth is a swot and a techie. Her dad is a
super-boffin who runs the Government's
Inventing Taskforce (GIT). She's inherited
his absented-minded braininess. She's not
so hot on the practical side of things
though — she can design a robot to tie your
shoelaces, but she's always tripping over
her own feet. She comes to school on her
rocket-powered rollerblades.

A Passion for Excellence

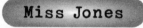
Miss Jones

Miss Jones is responsible for teaching
Class 3D the ordinary everyday subjects
like Maths and English and History. She's
newly-qualified, quiet and unassuming.
Like Miss Jones, all the subject teachers
at Thunder Raker Manor are fully
qualified and at the very peak of their
profession. Many of them are former
agents and spies, so together they bring
a wealth of experience to the school.

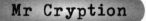
Mr Cryption

Mr Cryption — teaches Codes.
He's tall and thin and no one
understands anything he says.

Miss Fortune teaches Assassination. Her classes always seem to be a few pupils short — they get sent on errands or asked to help fetch something, and never come back... Note, though, that Class 3D is too young for Assassination, which is only taught in the Sixth Form.

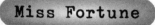

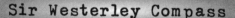

Sir Westerley Compass

Sir Westerly Compass is in charge of Tracking Skills. He's always late for class, and his lessons are often moved at short notice.

The Major

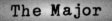

The Major — that's all he's ever called — is in charge of Sabotage Training. He has an enormous moustache and he's rather accident prone. Everything he touches breaks — even the plate he gets his school dinner on...

Mrs Nuffink

Mrs Nuffink teaches Surveillance. Don't mess around in her class — she's got eyes in the back of her head. No, really.

Mr Trick

Camouflage is supposed to be taught by Mr Trick. But no one can find him.

Reverend "Bongo" Smithers

The Chaplain is Reverend "Bongo" Smithers, a former fighter pilot more interested in war stories than Bible stories. He also teaches PE. Ruthlessly.

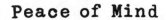

Top Secret

Peace of Mind

So whatever your parental requirements or security clearance, you can rest assured that Thunder Raker Manor will provide a first class education for your child in every respect. We can't tell you how much the children enjoy being here. No, really — we can't. It's an official secret.

Chapter I

Alfie's dad had a very ordinary name. Loads and loads of people had exactly the same name. In fact, one of those people who had the same very ordinary name was the Prime Minister.

And that was how the misunderstanding happened.

When Alfie's dad got a new job and the whole family moved house, Alfie's parents wanted him to go to the very best school in the area, a school where he would be happy and would learn lots.

One morning, while Alfie was eating his cornflakes and his mum was making toast, Alfie's dad came home from work. This was not as strange as it might sound, because Alfie's dad was a postman so he started work very early and finished when Alfie and his mum were just starting their day.

Alfie's dad dropped his postman's cap on the table beside Alfie's cornflakes and declared, "I've found it."

"Your cap?" Alfie asked. "I didn't know you'd lost it."

"No," said Dad. "I have found your new school."

The cornflakes in Alfie's mouth became a

spray of soggy breakfast that spattered across Dad's cap. "School?!"

"You have to go to school," Dad pointed out. "Ask your mother."

"Mum?" Alfie said.

"You have to go to school," Mum said. "Ask your dad."

Alfie sighed.

"What's the school like?" Alfie's mum asked.

Alfie's dad sat down and helped himself to a slice of toast. "It's a strange looking place. I didn't realise it even was a school until this morning. Their post comes in a special sealed bag. I just hand it to a man in uniform at the gate. He has a hat too, very official."

"Where is it?" Alfie asked.

"On his head, of course," said Alfie's dad.

"I think he means the school," Mum said. "Not the hat."

"Oh. It's just up the road. The big old house behind the electric fences and security gates."

"I thought that was a government place," Mum said. "Secret."

"No," Dad assured her. "It's a school. I know that because their special post bag is labelled 'Thunder Raker Manor School'."

"Weird name," Alfie said. But he wasn't surprised: he'd seen the big house Dad was talking about and *it* was pretty weird too. He wasn't sure if he wanted to go to a school that had security gates and electric fences round it. He was a quiet boy who liked to keep himself to himself and not cause or get into trouble. Security gates and electric fences sounded like trouble.

"The man at the gate says it's the best school of its kind in the country, maybe in the world," Dad said proudly. "And it's in *our* neighbourhood. And I think we should send Alfie there."

"But it looks weird," Alfie said, very quietly.

Dad didn't seem to hear him, and Mum was buttering more toast. "Good," she said. "The new term starts next week, so I'm glad that's all sorted."

That afternoon, Alfie's dad wrote a letter. He addressed it to *The Head Teacher, Thunder*

Raker Manor School. The next day he would slip the letter into the special post bag before he handed it to the man at the gate.

Alfie's dad signed the letter with his name – his very ordinary and not at all unusual name that he just happened to share with the Prime Minister. And because Alfie's dad knew that his name was very ordinary and not at all unusual, he put in brackets after it the letters "PM", for Post Man, so that the Head Teacher would be sure to know who the letter had come from.

And that's how the misunderstanding really got going.

"Come in, come in," called Mr Trenchard, the head teacher of Thunder Raker Manor, when Miss Jones knocked on his door. He peered at her suspiciously over a pair of wire-framed spectacles. "Who are you?" he asked.

"I'm Miss Jones."

Mr Trenchard gave a funny sort of cough. "Never heard of you. What do you want?"

"You sent for me, Mr Trenchard."

He tried looking at her through the spectacles, in case that made any difference. "Why would I do that?" he said.

"I teach Class 3D," Miss Jones said patiently.

This was not the first time Mr Trenchard had claimed not to know her. "Miss Jones, remember?"

Mr Trenchard considered this. "Are you wearing a disguise?"

"No."

"Is that beard real, then?"

Miss Jones frowned. She was a young lady who considered herself to be rather attractive. "I don't have a beard."

"Ah, so it's a *false* one then. Oh, no, hang on, my mistake." Mr Trenchard pulled off his spectacles and examined them carefully. "Bit of fluff on my glasses."

He gave them a polish on the sleeve of his jacket. "There, that's better. Now, I'm glad you're here, because I've had this letter," – he picked it up and waved it about vigorously – "from the PM – the *Prime Minister*. So it's probably very secret. Best way to deal with secrets, I find, is to forget them straight away. I used to practice that when I was younger, you know. I got to be terribly good at forgetting things. Do it all the time now. Just goes to show what practice can do." Mr Trenchard nodded happily. "I'm good at forgetting things too," he said proudly.

"So what does the letter say?" Miss Jones asked.

Mr Trenchard looked blank.

"The letter in your hand, from the PM," Miss Jones said.

"Ah, yes, very important." Mr Trenchard brandished the letter excitedly. "The Prime Minister wants us to take a new boy, a lad called Alfie. Must be a pretty special chap if the PM has written personally to tell us about him. He will start next week when the new term begins." Mr Trenchard clicked his tongue. "Didn't realise the old term had ended actually," he muttered. "Oh well. Anyway, yes. Alfie – he'll be in Class 3D. Don't suppose you know who teaches that class?"

"Yes," Miss Jones said. "*I* do."

"Really?" Mr Trenchard said. "Lucky you were here then."

"Isn't it just?" Miss Jones said quietly as she left the room.

Chapter 2

Alfie was a very ordinary boy. And like any ordinary boy starting at a new school, he was a bit nervous as he walked from home that first morning of term. There didn't seem to be any other local children walking to school. But he saw other children being taken to school by their parents.

A large, black car with little flags on the sides of the bonnet swept past Alfie. The windows were so dark he couldn't see in, but a smudge on the glass might just have been a girl's nose pressed hard against the window as she looked out. The smudge moved to keep track of Alfie as the car went by.

Further up the road, a helicopter passed over Alfie's head then swooped noisily down and headed in the direction of Thunder Raker Manor School. Alfie could see it hovering over the grounds. Ropes dropped down from the open side of the helicopter and several dark figures slid down them to the roof.

Alfie was just turning into the road that led to the school when he heard the rumble of an engine. It grew louder, and Alfie saw with surprise that a huge armoured tank was driving up the road towards him. Poking up from the turret was the top half of a man in army uniform wearing thick goggles. The man saluted Alfie as the tank went past, the whole road shaking under its weight. Behind the tank the tarmac was churned up by its tracks.

"It's the same every time term starts," a voice said as the tank rumbled into the distance.

Alfie looked round and saw a little old lady standing by the gate of a small cottage set back from the road. Her white hair was tied up in a bun on the back of her head and she had smiling, friendly eyes.

"Noise and upset," she said, shaking her head. "The council will have to resurface the road you know. Again."

"Oh, dear," Alfie said. He felt uncomfortable now the lady was talking to him. But he couldn't just walk away.

"Not to worry," she said. "I don't mind the school too much. It's nice to hear the sound of children playing nearby."

From the direction of the school came the dull *crump* of an explosion.

"Reminds me of when I was young," she said.

Alfie thought he could hear machine gun fire now. "I'm Alfie," he said loudly, over the noise.

"Mrs Prendergast," the old lady said. "Haven't seen you go past before, have I?"

"I'm new, starting today."

Mrs Prendergast nodded. "That'll be why then. Usually it's just those men in the black overalls and dark glasses hiding in the shrubbery and taking pictures of the school." She sniffed. "I give them cups of tea, but they don't seem very pleased. Oh, well, nice to talk to you. I must put the kettle on."

On his way to the school's big iron gates, Alfie was passed by several more large cars, an armoured personnel carrier and a girl in a pink helmet and goggles on roller skates.

The roller skates had jets of flame coming out of them and the girl shot past faster than the cars. She gave Alfie a wave as he jumped back out of the way. Then she wobbled and shot off even faster. The uniformed man dragged the gates open just in time for her to zoom through. Black smoke trailed after her.

Alfie emerged from the cloud of smoke to find himself at the gate. The guard looked down at him.

"I'm here for the start of school," Alfie explained.

The guard was holding a clipboard and examined a piece of paper attached to it. "Name?" he demanded.

"Alfie."

The guard's frown turned into a smile. "Alfie – welcome to Thunder Raker." He tucked the clipboard under his arm and shook the surprised Alfie by the hand. "I'm sure you'll be very happy here, but anything you need – anything at all…" He winked at Alfie. "Just ask. Any problems, come to me. Sergeant Custer."

"Thank you."

Alfie wondered where he was supposed to

go, but before he could summon the courage to ask, Sergeant Custer showed him the way to reception. "They'll be waiting for you," he assured Alfie. "Oh, and if you happen to be speaking to You-Know-Who..." He winked again, and tapped his nose.

Alfie didn't know who You-Know-Who could be, and he felt confused and embarrassed.

"You *know*," Sergeant Custer insisted. He leaned down and whispered a name in Alfie's ear.

"But that's my dad," Alfie said in surprise.

Sergeant Custer looked surprised too. He straightened up quickly and saluted. "It's all right," he told Alfie, looking round quickly to check they couldn't be overheard. "Your secret is safe with me."

Alfie followed the drive up to the large, imposing house that was Thunder Raker Manor. The front door was standing open and an elderly man with a beaked nose introduced himself as Mr Trenchard the Head Teacher. He told Alfie he was very welcome, and that Alfie should spend his time at the school wisely. He should learn as much as he could, and then forget it all. For "security reasons".

Alfie wasn't quite sure how it would help to forget everything he learned, but he didn't like to ask. At that moment a young woman arrived and introduced herself as his teacher, Miss Jones.

"Goodbye, Mr Trenchard," Alfie said as he followed Miss Jones along to meet Class 3D.

"Goodbye, er, that boy," Mr Trenchard called after him.

"He forgets everything," Miss Jones told Alfie. "Makes a point of it."

"Why?" Alfie asked.

"I don't think he can remember," Miss Jones replied. She had to shout to be heard over the roaring of some kind of engine. The noise got louder as she opened the door to the classroom. "Now, come in and meet the rest of your class."

Chapter 3

The engine noise was even louder inside and the classroom was full of dark smoke.

"Beth!" Miss Jones shouted. "If it's you making that racket, then stop it now."

With the door open, the smoke began to thin and clear. Alfie could see there were half a dozen children in the room, most of them sitting at their desks. The exception was the girl in the pink helmet whom Alfie had seen on his way to school. The flames at the back of her roller skates faded and died as the jet engines coughed and spluttered to a halt. But she was still moving very fast, circling the desks. A fair-haired boy in a wheelchair reversed rapidly out of her way as she passed.

"Sorry, Miss – no brakes!" the girl yelled as she shot by.

Miss Jones grabbed the girl's shoulders and was dragged along for several metres before they both skidded to a halt. The soles of the teacher's shoes were smoking, and there was a strong smell of burnt rubber.

"Thank you, Beth," Miss Jones said. "Now if you will please put those skates in the stock cupboard and sit down, I'd like to introduce Alfie, who's joining Class 3D today."

"Wicked," shouted a boy with close-cut dark hair. "Can Alfie sit by me, Miss? Can he? Please?"

"We'll sort out where Alfie sits in a minute," Miss Jones told the boy. She waited for Beth to sit down. Under her helmet, Alfie saw that Beth had brown hair that was cut into the same exact shape, so it looked like she still had the helmet on.

"Right, then," Miss Jones said, "I think we should all introduce ourselves."

A smug-looking girl with dark hair and glasses cleared her throat and stood up. She looked at Alfie suspiciously. "I'm Chloe," she said. "And my dad is just *so* important. He's a spy, but obviously I can't tell you his name or where he is. But I expect you know all about him anyway, he's just so famous." She looked expectantly at Alfie.

"No, sorry," he said.

Chloe went as pink as Beth's helmet and sat down. She glared at Alfie.

The boy with short dark hair laughed and Miss Jones pointed at him. "Jack."

Jack stood up. "I'm Jack and my dad's far

more important than Chloe's. During the holidays we went to Russia because Dad has to go to meetings at the Kremlin with the President and other important people. I worked out how they could keep the streets clear of snow and ice, but Dad said it would cost too much."

Next was the fair-haired boy in the wheelchair. One arm of the wheelchair opened and a clipboard with notes on it popped up on a metal rod. He read out loud from the notes. "I'm Sam. My mum works at the Hush-Hush Department inventing stuff for agents. She made my wheelchair because the NHS one didn't have a very good anti-missile protection system. And one of the wheels was wonky."

Alfie tried his best not to look puzzled, because he didn't want to look stupid in front of his new class. But it seemed to him that this was the most peculiar bunch of children he had ever met.

Then Beth stood up. She had taken off the jet-skates and was now wearing a pair of ordinary looking trainers. "I'm Beth and I invent stuff. My dad's in the Government Inventing Taskforce." She paused and sniffed. "That's GIT to you," she said to Chloe, who scowled and looked away. "Anyway, I have my own laboratory and everything and I've designed tons of great stuff including a robot that can tie your shoelaces."

"She brought it in for show and tell," Sam said. "It tied her shoelaces together and she fell over."

"That is not true," Beth shouted. "Alice tripped me up."

"Did not," said the last of the girls. She was short and thin with long blonde hair.

"Never in a million years. And if I did, you deserved it. So there." She caught Miss Jones's severe look and stood up. "Anyway, I'm Alice. My dad's a double-double agent." She frowned and checked on her fingers. "Or it might be double-double-double. It gets very confusing."

"Isn't that a triple-double?" the last of the boys asked.

"No," Alice snapped back. "That's just stupid. How can you be so stupid, Harry? It might be a double-triple, but whoever heard of a triple-double?"

"You next, Harry," Miss Jones said quickly.

Harry stood up. He was a large boy – taller and broader than Alfie. "Harry," he said. "I like PE best. And the assault course." He started to sit down again, then changed his mind and stopped halfway between standing and sitting. "Oh, and my dad's infiltrated SPUD. Again."

There was a hushed silence.

"Really?" Sam said, impressed.

"You can't tell us that," Jack hissed in a loud whisper.

"Yeah," Chloe told him. "And *you* can't tell us your dad is head of the Secret Service, but you do."

"Never!" Jack shot back.

"Like, all the time," Alice said.

Miss Jones held her hands up for silence. "Alfie," she said, "why don't you tell us a little bit about yourself?"

Alfie was still trying to make sense of what

everyone else had said. "SPUD," he said at last. "Isn't that a potato?"

"Hey – good one!" Jack said. "Alfie thinks Harry's dad's a potato!"

"Don't be silly," Sam said from his wheelchair. "Alfie thinks Harry's dad has *infiltrated* a potato."

"With a knife and fork?" Beth suggested.

"Children!" Miss Jones shouted above the noise. "Please – we are welcoming a new member of Class 3D. Alfie was about to tell us about himself."

"So what's your dad do, Alfie?" Chloe asked. "Bet he's not as important as *my* dad."

Alfie looked at her. He looked at all the children, staring back at him expectantly. He felt nervous and alone and it was a struggle to say anything at all. "Well, actually," he said at last, "my dad's a postman."

The class collapsed into laughter. Even Miss Jones was having trouble keeping a straight face. "I can see you have a great sense of humour, Alfie," she said. "You'll fit in just fine with Class 3D."

Chapter 4

Miss Jones taught Alfie's class all the ordinary subjects that Alfie recognised and remembered from his previous school. Class 3D stayed in the same room with her for Maths and Literacy, for reading and for history topic work. But for other lessons they had other teachers, and went to those teachers' classrooms.

Alfie tagged along with the other three boys in his class – Jack, Harry and Sam, whose wheelchair was motorised so no one had to push it. "Mum fitted a turbo boost during the holidays," Sam said quietly. "But don't tell Beth. I'm going to race her on her roller skates at afternoon break."

"Why not do it now?" Harry asked.

"Better not. From top speed, it takes me a hundred metres to stop."

"So what's this SPUD thing if it isn't a potato?" Alfie asked when the others had stopped talking.

"You really don't know?" Jack said.

"I really don't know," Alfie admitted. "Sorry."

"Actually no one knows who they are," said Sam. "But we do know that SPUD stands for Secret Partners for Undertaking Destruction. They're the bad guys."

"My dad..." Harry began slowly. Then he stopped. "Nothing," he said quickly.

Jack slapped him on the shoulder. "It's all right, we know."

"This is a very strange school," Alfie said quietly.

Alice had come up behind them. "Isn't it?" she agreed. "It's great! So, your dad's a postman?"

"That's right."

Alice shook her head in obvious admiration. "What a fantastic cover story. I mean, a secret identity and everything. Wicked!"

The next lesson was Codes. Alfie thought that might be about how to find books in the school library, or maybe something to do with programming computers. He liked libraries and he liked computers. You could work quietly and on your own with both.

"It should be double Camouflage now," Alice told him. "That's taught by Mr Trick."

"I'm the absolute best at Camouflage," Chloe said loudly. "But we haven't had it all year."

"Why not?"

Chloe looked at Alfie like he was mad and he knew she was still annoyed at him from earlier. "No one can find Mr Trick."

Codes was taught by Mr Cryption. He was a tall thin man who beckoned them all into the classroom with an extendable metal rod like a radio aerial that he waved and pointed.

Alfie sat at the same table as Jack. "Shouldn't we have books or paper or something?"

Jack shook his head. "No need. You wouldn't know what to do with them anyway."

"Why not?"

But before Jack could answer, Mr Cryption started the lesson. "Xylophonics," he announced in a loud voice.

"Pig dawn over testament in Arcadia est."

"That's why," Jack said. "None of us know what he's on about."

Mr Cryption glared at Jack. "Fester block

garden tailor vision," he warned. "Visible run dilemma phoenix fin passion on gold identity submarine."

"Are all the lessons like that?" Alfie asked as they moved on to the next class. He was beginning to worry about the sort of homework he might get.

"Not all of them," Beth assured him. "Mr Cryption is just strange."

"That bit about the trombones was interesting," Harry said.

They reached the next classroom to find a notice taped to the door. Alice read it out: "Class 3D – Go to Room 11F." She sighed. "Not again!"

"Where's Room 11F?" Alfie asked.

"Miles away," Sam told him. "Typical."

"Why's the lesson been moved?"

"Because it's Tracking Skills," Chloe said. She folded her arms and glared at Alfie. "Something else I'm good at. And I bet you're rubbish at it."

"It's always moved," Alice said before Alfie could respond. "Never where it's supposed to be."

Room 11F had another notice on the door sending them to 17C, where they were directed again to the main school hall. But when Jack opened the door to the hall, there was another class in there already.

Alfie watched in amazement as a large man in a black cloak ran round the hall making aeroplane noises, his cloak spread out behind him like wings as he ran. Children leaped out of his way. *"Dugger-dugger-dugger,"* went the man, making the sound of a machine gun.

Jack closed the door.

"Who was that?" Alfie asked.

"It's just the Chaplain, Reverend Smithers," Alice said.

"What is he teaching, running about like that?"

"He used to be a fighter pilot," Harry said. "He takes us for PE."

"Was that PE?"

Chloe looked at Alfie like he was mad again. "That was Religious Studies," she said.

They never did find where their Tracking Skills lesson was being held. It was supposed to be taught by Sir Waverly Compass, but no one had seen him since he set off for the kitchens to get a pint of milk for the Staff Room.

Chapter 5

Top Secret

On the way to lunch, Jack suddenly grabbed Alfie and pulled him to the side of the corridor.

"Look out!" he hissed.

Alfie struggled to see what was going on, but the corridor was empty – apart from the rest of his class pressed against the walls, and a harmless-looking lady with greying hair who was walking slowly towards them.

"It's Miss Fortune," Sam explained,

keeping his wheelchair as close to the wall as it would go. Up close, Alfie could see there were buttons arranged along both arms. Sam pressed one, and the chair scrunched up so that it took up less room.

"Miss Fortune teaches Assassination Techniques," Chloe said. "Why don't you go and say hello to her?"

But before Chloe had finished speaking, the harmless-looking lady let out a high-pitched wail: "Hai-char!" and leaped suddenly into the air. Her right foot lashed out and Alfie saw that there was a hollow tube extending from the point of her shoe. Smoke and flame erupted from the tube – a gun barrel – and a chunk of wall close to where Alice was standing exploded into dust and fragments.

Miss Fortune settled back on her feet, the gun barrel shrank out of sight and she walked slowly past the children of Class 3D.

"Good afternoon," she said in a frail-sounding voice. Then she spun round on her heel, smacking a fist out rapidly at Harry, who ducked just in time.

"It's best to keep out of her way," Beth said to Alfie. "Whatever Chloe says."

"What are her lessons like?" Alfie wondered as Miss Fortune disappeared round a corner in the corridor.

Jack waited for the blood-curdling sound of a ninja attack cry to fade before he said: "No idea. We don't do Assassination Techniques until the sixth form. But the Major once told me her classes always seem to be short of pupils."

"She sent Felix Hamilton to get something from the stock cupboard and he never came back," Alice said darkly. "And Sarah Middlesworth."

"I heard it was Lester Bigmore," Sam said.

"Yeah. Him too," Alice said.

"Who's the Major?" Alfie asked.

"You need to keep out of his way as well," Jack said. "He teaches Sabotage. We have that on Wednesday afternoon. Just before Maths."

Alfie met the Major at lunch. No one seemed to know what his name was – he was just "The Major". He was a straight-backed, military-looking man with a bushy white moustache that stuck out beyond his cheeks in a way that defied gravity. He also had his left arm in a sling and several plasters stuck on his cheek.

Jack pointed out the Major as he was getting a plate of stew to take to the table where the staff were having their lunch. Alfie watched each of the teachers sit down and take it in turns to introduce themselves to Mr Trenchard as if he'd never met them before.

But the Major didn't get that far. As he turned from the serving area, his sling caught on one of the metal struts supporting the raised shelf where the plates were kept warm. The strut fell away and one end of the shelf dropped with a loud clang. But it was nothing like as loud as the plates as they slipped down the shelf and crashed to the floor.

"Sorry!" the Major said loudly to no one in particular as he knocked a small girl flying, then bumped into a table. Which collapsed,

sending dinners and drinks into the air.

"Uh-oh – me again!" the Major said, so loudly that a passing boy stumbled and clutched his ears, dropping the jug of water he was carrying.

"That wasn't me," the Major said, looking down at the puddle and the broken glass. "Er, was it?"

"Like I said," Jack whispered to Alfie, "the Major teaches Sabotage."

"I see," Alfie replied, watching the Major set his dinner down carefully on the table. There was

a crack as the plate broke. The Major sat
down. His chair fell apart beneath him.

There was only one lesson in the afternoon
before the class returned to Miss Jones. It was
Surveillance. This was taught by Mrs Nuffink,
and Alfie found it the hardest lesson of the
day.

This was partly because Mrs Nuffink
seemed to be able to tell if anyone whispered
or wasn't paying attention, or mucked about.
Even when she was facing the other way,
writing on the board, she called out: "Beth –

don't do that," as an expertly designed paper plane glided across Alfie's desk.

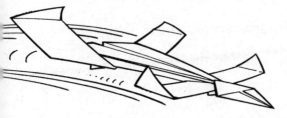

Alfie also found it hard because the subject was quite difficult. They spent a lot of time examining photographs and trying to spot where people could be hiding, or watching a video of the outside of a house where nothing seemed to be happening.

"There – did you see it?" Mrs Nuffink shrieked at one point. "Nobody? None of you saw anything? I despair, I really do. Class 3D, what were you doing?"

As far as Alfie could tell, nothing had happened.

But then Mrs Nuffink rewound the DVD. "I'll play it forward very slowly," she said with a sigh. "Look out for the boy delivering a secret letter."

There was a slight blur on the picture for a moment, but otherwise nothing changed.

"I didn't see anything," Alfie said.

"You wouldn't," Chloe said. But the others all agreed they had seen nothing either.

Mrs Nuffink shook her head sadly. "You'll never pass your SATS at this rate," she said. "Special Agent Training Standards are very important, and you need to get Level 3 this year. Now – one frame at a time then."

This time, they did see it. On one frame there was nothing, then on the next a boy was clearly in view. He was only in three frames. In the first, he approached the front of the house. In the second he threw a letter towards

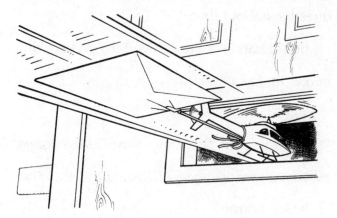

the door. In the third, Alfie could see that the letter was attached to a tiny model helicopter that flew it straight into the open letterbox. He could also see that the boy was on a skateboard. Flames erupted from the rocket motors on the back of the board as the boy whizzed past.

By the fourth frame he was gone.

"You see?" Mrs Nuffink said. "You just have to pay attention. Now then – any questions about that?"

Beth's hand shot up. "Yes, Miss. Where did he get that skateboard?"

"How was your first day, Alfie?" Miss Jones asked as she dismissed Class 3D at the end of the afternoon.

"I like the other children in Class 3D," Alfie said, though he was sure that Chloe didn't like him very much. "But some of the lessons are a bit strange."

"You'll get used to it," Miss Jones said.

"Probably. See you tomorrow. Oh, and you have PE in the afternoon, so don't forget to bring in your towel, your trainers, and your bullet-proof vest."

Chapter 6

Mum wanted to know if Alfie needed any help with his homework. He told her he could manage, thanks, but he needed a bullet-proof vest for PE the next day.

"Funny boy," Mum said, and ruffled Alfie's hair.

"It's an odd school," Alfie told his parents as they sat down for tea.

"You've only been there a day," Dad said. "It's bound to seem a bit strange."

"I suppose." But Alfie wasn't sure. "Do you

think they have special schools where the children of secret agents and spies and people like that go?" he asked.

"To keep them safe from the enemy?" Dad said. "And teach them all the secret stuff they might need to know to survive in the dangerous undercover world of international espionage?"

"Well, yes."

Alfie's dad paused. "I doubt it," he said.

"But if we hear of a school like that," Mum said, "we'll be sure to put your name down for it." And she winked at Dad, thinking that Alfie couldn't see her.

"For my homework," Alfie said slowly, "I have to draw up a plan for infiltrating a secret enemy military base, sabotaging the tracking system, stealing some vital plans and escaping through the minefield. Before the guard dogs get me."

"That's nice," Mum said.

"Good morning, Mrs Prendergast," Alfie called as he walked past the old lady's cottage the next morning.

Mrs Prendergast stood in the garden holding a tray with a teapot and milk jug on it. As she turned and waved to Alfie he just caught sight of a tall man in dark overalls and sunglasses disappearing into the bushes behind her. The man was holding a mug.

If Mrs Prendergast called back to Alfie, he didn't hear. It sounded like a rocket was fast approaching, as a swirl of smoke raced towards him. He hurried to the side of the road to let Beth shoot past.

She skidded and screeched to a halt just past Alfie and he ran to catch her up. She wasn't wearing roller skates today, but was on a skateboard like the boy had on the surveillance video.

"I thought it looked neat, so I made this one last night," she said.

"Didn't you do your homework?"

Beth grinned. "Chips did it for me."

"Is he your brother?" Alfie wondered.

"No, silly. He's my computer. Do you have a computer?"

Alfie shook his head. "Dad lets me use his if I need to. I don't even have a games console."

"Don't tell Chloe," Beth said. "She has all the latest kit. She's got a Playstation 7, a Z-Box, a Wii Mark 9, and the new Omni-Processing Decryptotron. Lucky thing." Beth adjusted her helmet strap. "See you." And in a blur of speed and a curl of smoke, she was gone.

Alfie passed three more men in dark

overalls hiding in the hedges outside the school. He pretended not to notice them as they whispered and murmured into radio handsets and drank tea. Sergeant Custer opened the gates for Alfie and snapped a neat salute.

"Dad says you can come and play after school one day if you want," Jack told Alfie as soon as he got into the classroom. "Once you've been positively vetted, of course. There's a form you need to fill in."

Miss Jones arrived before Alfie could reply. "There's a special assembly this morning," she announced. "Mr Trenchard has some important information."

They went to the school hall but Mr Trenchard

told them he didn't know who they were or why they were there, and could they all please go away and leave him in peace.

"Ah, no, hang on a minute," Mr Trenchard's voice boomed down the main corridor as they left.

No one seemed at all surprised by this, but simply turned round and trooped back into the hall.

"Right, good," Mr Trenchard said. He was holding a piece of paper and staring at it over the top of his spectacles. He stood at a lectern on the stage at the end of the hall. The other teachers sat on chairs behind him. "Important information here. Everyone pay attention."

"We're lucky he can remember how to read," Sam said as he edged his wheelchair into the gap between Alfie and Harry.

"Now," Mr Trenchard was saying, "we all know that SPUD has been trying to infiltrate the Service and get hold of our advanced technology." He paused and pushed his glasses up his nose. "Do we know that? Yes, I suppose we do. Might have slipped our minds but yes, indeed." He cleared his throat and went on: "Now, those boffins at the Government Inventing Taskforce…"

"GIT!" someone shouted from halfway down the hall.

"Absolutely," Mr Trenchard agreed. "Those boffins at GIT have got a spy satellite in a spot of bother up in orbit. Or rather, out of orbit." He paused to check his sheet of notes. "That is to say, it crashed to earth. Yesterday. And SPUD would

like nothing better than to get their hands on it."

"Why is that?" the Major asked.

"Because it's secret, that's why."

The Major nodded. "I see." His chair lurched precariously to the side as one of its legs fell off.

"Now the GIT chappies did manage to arrange for their satellite to crash just about...

here." Mr Trenchard frowned and re-checked his notes. "Well, not *here* exactly, in this hall, but somewhere in the local area. So it's up to us to recover it before SPUD agents move in and find it."

"Terrific," Jack whispered. "A real mission at last."

"Could be dangerous," Harry said quietly.

Jack nodded excitedly. "I know!"

"Each class will be given a different area to search," Mr Trenchard said. "If the satellite turns out to be in your area, your task is to recover it and bring it back here at once. Now, any questions?"

"What's it called?" a tall boy near the front asked.

"Apparently it's called Nigel," Mr Trenchard said. "Oh, no, hang on – that's the man who sent me this email. Who'd call a satellite by a person's name? What a silly idea." He inspected the sheet more closely. "Ah, here we are. It's actually our new Remote Orbital Satellite Information Equipment. Or ROSIE, for short. Any more questions?"

Mr Cryption cleared his throat, and asked: "Flammable geography rewind heart-shaped cashflow butter antelopes?"

Mr Trenchard nodded. "Very good question. The answer, without a shadow of doubt, is *Wednesday*. Now then, everyone back to your classrooms where your teachers will handle your mission briefings."

He had almost finished speaking when Miss Fortune leaped from her chair, clenched her fists, and with a cry of "Geronimo!" threw herself off the stage into the unsuspecting audience. The hall cleared very quickly.

Chapter 7

There were groans of disappointment when Miss Jones told Class 3D that the Upper School would be doing most of the work to find the satellite.

"But we've got PE this afternoon," Harry complained. "Can't we look for it then?"

"Well, there's nothing to stop you, although the Chaplain would have to agree." Miss Jones clapped her hands together. "But first we have double Science. I'd like you to carry on with your projects, please. Alfie – you can help Beth."

The other children in Class 3D were attaching wires to light bulbs and batteries and buzzers. The lights lit and the buzzers buzzed. But Beth was working on something rather more complicated.

She tipped a mass of wires and cables and circuits and electrical components out of a shoebox and started to plug them all together.

"What are we making?" Alfie asked as he held a wire for her.

"It was going to be a machine to tell you when your toast is done," Beth said. "When it's ready, a buzzer sounds and a light comes on. Miss Jones said we had to build something with buzzers and lights."

"Why not just use a toaster?" Alfie asked. "The toast pops up when it's done."

"Because it doesn't flash and buzz," Beth pointed out. "Anyway, I'm changing it. It's not going to be anything to do with toast."

"Then what is it?" Alfie asked. But when he saw Beth's wide grin, he guessed: "It's a satellite detector, isn't it?"

"Don't tell Miss Jones," Beth said quietly. "Or the Chaplain. We'll test it in PE."

"Won't the Chaplain notice?" Alfie asked.

"We'll have to hide it. Though it will be a bit big. And it will only detect the satellite when it's very close, so we need to make it portable."

"Too big and heavy to carry?"

Beth nodded.

Looking at the device that was starting to take shape, Alfie had an idea. "Why don't we build it into Sam's wheelchair?"

If the Chaplain noticed that Sam's wheelchair now had various wires and attachments added, along with a tall radio aerial, he didn't mention it. He was probably too busy talking about how children today had it easy and it was never like this in Bomber Command.

"I thought you were a fighter pilot not a bomber, sir?" Harry said.

"That too," the Chaplain barked. "Intrepid pilot. Went on a hundred and three sorties in one month alone. Survived 97 of them. Jerry never knew what was going to happen to him next, I can tell you."

"Jerry?" Alfie said.

"My co-pilot, Jerry Atkins," the Chaplain explained. "Right then, today I've arranged a short assault course for you."

Several people groaned.

"It won't be difficult," the Chaplain went on. "Just twice round the field, then climb over those bales of hay over there. It'll make men of you."

"I don't want to be a man," Alice said.

The Chaplain peered at her. "Ah, yes. People then. Oh," he remembered, "and you'll have to crawl under that wire mesh over there."

"Doesn't sound too bad," Alfie whispered to Jack.

"Avoiding the machine gun fire," the Chaplain continued. "Then it's a quick swing over the pond on the rope I've attached to that overhanging branch."

"Well, at least that should be all right," Jack said.

"Being careful not to fall in and get eaten by the hundred or so piranha fish I've put in the pond."

As Alfie and the others watched, a duck flew down towards the pond. It hovered just above the water before landing, and gave out a contented quack. Then a blue lightning bolt of electricity zapped up and hit the duck, which fell lifeless into the water.

"And the electric eel," the Chaplain went on. He hesitated as he saw Class 3D was looking past him, their mouths open. "Problem?"

The skeleton of a dead duck was tossed out of the pond and landed on the grass nearby.

"Good," said the Chaplain. "Right – off you go then."

Sam was allowed to whiz round the course in his wheelchair, since he couldn't crawl under the mesh or swing on the rope.

Beth's satellite detector bleeped and booped as he moved.

Alfie and Beth kept close to Sam. "Any sign of it yet?" asked Alfie.

"Nothing so far." Sam waited while Beth and Alfie ducked under the mesh and crawled quickly through. The ground exploded round them.

"See if you can move out a bit," Alfie suggested. "Cover a bigger area."

After they'd swung successfully over the pond, Alfie turned to Beth. "How close does the detector need to be to find the satellite?"

Beth sighed. "It's not easy to get long range with a portable, battery-powered detector you know."

"How close?"

"About a metre."

Alfie frowned. "But that means Sam will have to run over it."

"Maybe." Beth looked a bit embarrassed.

"Wouldn't he see it first?"

"Maybe," she said again.

As he watched Sam whizzing back and forth across the playground at twenty miles an hour, Alfie wasn't sure that Beth's detector was going to be the best way to find the satellite after all.

Chapter 8

Top Secret

"That was very good, Alfie," Miss Jones said as she handed back his homework the next morning. "In fact, yours was the only plan that the Homework Analysis Team gave a 90% chance of success."

"What did you do?" Jack wanted to know. "I only got a 45% chance of success. I never heard of anyone getting 90%."

"Did you pole vault over the electric fences?" Sam wanted to know.

"Stun the guard dogs with an electric shock gun you invented yourself?" Beth asked.

"Maybe he dug a tunnel," Alice suggested.

"I did."

"No," Chloe told them, "a powered hang-glider with sat-nav is best. My dad bought me one the other week. Bet you didn't think of that," she told Alfie.

"I just shot all the guards and blew up the place," Harry said glumly. "HAT said that didn't fulfil the Mission Brief because I didn't get hold of the vital plans. Only gave me 10%."

"So come on," Jack said, "how did you do it?"

Alfie shrugged, embarrassed by all the attention. "I pretended to be a postman bringing the letters. Special delivery to be signed for by the chief scientist. That way they'd send me to the lab where I could sabotage the systems."

"And the plans?" Harry asked. "They'd search you on the way out."

"Put them in an envelope addressed to myself and left it in the letter tray to be sent out."

There was a long silence. Then Beth said:

"That's brilliant!" and Sam laughed and clapped.

Everyone else agreed, except Chloe who told them that the HAT assessors must have muddled up the papers and got Alfie's confused with hers.

"I still think my plan would have worked too," Jack muttered.

"It must have taken you all evening," Miss Jones said as she tried to settle Class 3D down again.

"Not really," Alfie said. "I still had time to find out where the missing satellite landed."

Mr Trenchard regarded Alfie through his spectacles. For once he didn't seem to need reminding of what was going on.

"Alfie," he said. "Settled in OK, I hope?"

"Yes, thank you, sir."

"Excellent. Wouldn't want any complaints getting back to..." Mr Trenchard leaned meaningfully across the table. "You-Know-Who," he whispered.

"No, I don't, actually," Alfie said.

But Mr Trenchard ignored this. "Now, Miss Smith – or is it Jones? Well, whoever it was has told me you know where this satellite thingy is."

"That's right. You see, my dad was talking to Mr Rogers in Willow Lane, and he said that Mrs Sykes had heard from the Oyanbanji boys that Mrs Green in the shop said old Mr Phillips got a dreadful fright the other night when something fell out of the sky."

Alfie had said all this in a rush and he didn't expect Mr Trenchard to follow, but to his surprise the Head Teacher nodded. "And did this Willow Lane character say what it was that fell from the sky?"

"Er, well," Alfie explained, "Dad spoke to old Mr Phillips and he said that yes he'd had a fright because a shooting star almost fell on him, and his dog ran off, and talking to Edward Hogsmouth he thought –

Mr Hogsmouth, not the dog – that it landed somewhere in Mrs Prendergast's back garden."

"I see." Mr Trenchard took off his glasses and polished them furiously on a grubby handkerchief. "Your dad's got quite a network of informers."

"They're just people who live nearby."

Mr Trenchard winked. "Course they are. So we reckon this satellite is in Mrs Prendergast's garden?"

"Yes," said Alfie.

"Thank goodness no one knows about it."

"Apart from old Mr Phillips," said Alfie.

"Well, yes, obviously."

"And Mrs Hogsmouth," Alfie added. "Oh and Mrs Green and the Oyanbanji boys and

Mr Rogers and Mrs Sykes. And Dad of course. And the dog."

"And this Willow fellow. But thank goodness no one *else* knows it's in this lady's garden. Where is the garden, by the way?"

"It's the one where the men in black overalls and dark glasses hide to keep watch on the school," said Alfie.

Mr Trenchard leaped to his feet. "Spies? Keeping watch on the school? They must be SPUD agents!"

"I don't know. Mrs Prendergast takes them cups of tea."

Mr Trenchard sniffed. "Consorting with the

enemy," he said darkly. Then he looked up suddenly. "Wait a minute. These SPUD agents – how often do they watch the school?"

"Every morning," said Alfie. "They use binoculars."

"Then maybe they have the satellite already. It's right under their noses."

Alfie shook his head. "I don't think so. They were still hiding and drinking tea this morning. One of them had a rich tea finger."

The Head Teacher nodded and steepled his fingers. "Excellent. Now then, Alfie, what's your plan for recovering the satellite?"

Alfie was surprised. "*My* plan?"

"You found the satellite, you know all about the SPUD agents and this collaborator woman, your homework was pretty good. You must have a plan. I'm turning this mission over to Class 3D at once."

There were cheers when Alfie told the class what had happened. Even Chloe looked pleased at the news. They decided to spend their morning break drawing up their plans.

"The first thing we must do," Beth said, "is use my detector to find exactly where the satellite is."

"It's quite a big back garden," Alfie agreed.

"Maybe the SPUD agents have already found it," Chloe said.

"Have they?" Alice asked Alfie.

He shook his head. "I don't think so. They were still hiding and drinking tea this morning."

"Doesn't sound like they know where to look then," Sam said.

"Or they were on a break," Chloe said.

"Either way," Jack said, "we need to stop them finding the satellite before we can get to it."

"We should take them out," Harry decided.

"Where to?" Alfie asked. "Maybe a tea shop? With biscuits?"

"No," Sam said, "Harry means shoot them."

"Is that a good idea?" Alice asked. "It might attract attention."

"I can make silencers for Sam's built-in

machine guns," Beth offered.

"But I was going to use the grenade launcher in the seat back and the rockets from between the wheels," Sam said.

"What do you think, Alfie?" Alice asked.

"Yes, come on Mr Clever Clogs," Chloe said.

"I think," Alfie said slowly, "that we need to get them out of Mrs Prendagast's garden. The best way to do that is to convince them that the satellite is really somewhere else."

"Terrific!" Jack exclaimed. "We stage a crash landing. Get another satellite to come down somewhere else and make sure they see it. We can hide nearby and make satellite-crashing noises in case they miss it." He demonstrated: "Neeeeeaaaaaooooow wwwww – booomph!"

"Or," said Alfie, "we could just dig a big hole and pretend we've already found it."

Chapter 9

By the end of the afternoon the older children from Upper School had dug a pit at the side of the playground well away from Mrs Prendergast's garden. The spot had been carefully chosen by Sir Waverly Compass. Since the Major had been taken off the digging party the sides of the pit hadn't collapsed and buried anyone at all.

Sergeant Custer was on guard, making as much noise as he could to make sure the

SPUD agents would realise there was something "going on". He marched up and down, shouting, "Who goes there?" and "Can't tell you, it's a secret but it's absolutely nothing at all whatsoever to do with any special satellites that might have crashed in this area recently, oh dear me no." Which was completely true.

To make the illusion as complete as possible, the Chaplain was organising a PE lesson with Class 11F on one side of the pit – a fairly routine session with skipping ropes, hoops, footballs and a savage Siberian tiger.

On the other side of the pit, Miss Fortune was teaching what was left of 10A. There had been nine children in her group when she started but they were now down to only three, who all looked rather nervous.

The men in black uniforms and dark glasses had been spotted hiding in the bushes at the edge of the playground. They watched closely, ready to move in as soon as they saw anything that looked like a secret satellite...

In their classroom, Class 3D had a picture of Mrs Prendergast's back garden projected onto the white board. It had been taken with a digital camera from a radio-controlled model plane that Beth had adapted to fly over the area. Until it passed over the Major as he

made his way from the digging to First Aid –
then it crashed in a ball of flame, singeing the
Major's eyebrows and blackening his face
with smoke.

"Can't see much," Harry complained.

"We really need to see it from closer up,"
Alfie said. "How high was the camera when it
took this?"

"Three miles," Beth said proudly.

"And the garden is that little dot just
there?" Alice checked.

"No, that's Birmingham. The garden is
here," Beth said, using her laser pointer. It
burned a hole through the board. "Or is it
over there?" The hole stretched into a smoking
line as she moved the pointer. "I wonder if I
have this turned up too high."

"Maybe we need a new plan to find exactly where the satellite is," Chloe said. "I think we've left it too much to Alfie."

"I've been working on a plan," Jack said proudly. He nodded to Sam.

One arm of Sam's wheelchair flipped open
and a metal rod extended upwards. Fixed to
the top was a rolled sheet of paper, which
dropped down. On the paper was a large
picture. Everyone looked at it in surprise.

"Isn't that..." Alfie said slowly, "...a badger?"

"Absolutely," said Jack. And here's the plan. Once we've identified the SCAR, then we can effect a TUF. The TABs will then use the TUF to reach the SCAR. The TABs will go into SET mode and Bob's your uncle. Any questions?"

Alice put her hand up. "What does BOB stand for?"

"It doesn't stand for anything. It's a saying. "Bob's your uncle." Bob is short for Robert. And it means everything is OK."

"So what does OK stand for?" Chloe asked.

"*My* uncle," Harry said slowly, "is called Derek."

"I think I got the Bob stuff," Alfie said, "but what was the other bit about?"

"Which other bit?" Jack asked.

"All of it. Can you say it again, please, slowly."

Jack took a deep breath. "Once… we… have… id… ent… if… ied…"

"Er, a bit quicker than that," Beth said.

"All right. Once we've identified the SCAR, then we can effect—"

"Hang on," Alfie said quickly. "What's a SCAR?"

"It's like, when you cut yourself," Sam said, "You know, on a sharp edge or maybe it's a scratch from a plant or something. Might be in the kitchen… Or even a burn will do it… I remember once, when my mum was out—"

"The SCAR," Jack said importantly, "is the Satellite Crash Area of Recovery."

"Right," Alfie said. "So, once we find where the satellite has crashed..."

"...then we can effect a TUF," Jack finished.

Alice opened her mouth to ask a question.

Jack sighed. "Tunnel Under the Fence," he explained. He shook his head sadly. "Don't any of you know anything? Right, after we tunnel under the fence, where Mrs Prendergast's garden borders the school grounds, then the TABs – that's the Trained Assault Badgers..."

Sam pointed to the big picture beside him. "Badgers," he confirmed.

"Yes, the badgers will use the TUF..."

"The tunnel under the fence," Alice said.

"That's right, they'll use the tunnel to reach the SCAR."

"The satellite," Harry said.

"Very good, yes. And they – the badgers – will go into SET mode."

"Is that the set where they live?" Alfie asked.

"No," Jack said. "It's Satellite Equipment Transfer mode. It means they'll bring it back to us."

"The badgers," Sam said, pointing to his picture again.

"Yes."

"Which we have trained," Harry said.

"Of course."

"Sorry," Harry said. "But, when did we do that?"

"Er," Jack said.

"Do we actually *have* any badgers?" Alfie asked.

"Maybe we could use the Chaplain's electric eel?" Alice suggested.

Sam shook his head. "I haven't got a picture of that."

"Robert might have one," Harry told him.

"Who is Robert?" Jack asked.

"I thought he was your uncle. Bob for short."

"So," Alfie said quickly, "apart from having no badgers, trained or not, and not knowing exactly where the satellite is in the garden, and not having dug a tunnel under the fence, it's a good plan."

"Thanks," said Jack, beaming. "Hey,

maybe the badgers could wear specially adapted cameras on their heads and search for the satellite when they get there."

"Do we have any specially adapted cameras?" Alfie asked.

"We've got as many as we have badgers," Beth told him.

"Then they can have one each," Harry said. "And we'll find the satellite in Mrs Prendergast's garden in no time."

"Or," Alfie said patiently, "we could borrow binoculars from Mrs Nuffink's Surveillance Classroom, and go up on the school roof and see if we can spot it from there."

Chloe sighed. "I thought it was someone else's turn to come up with a plan."

"I think it's a great idea!" Alice said. "We'll spot the satellite from the roof."

"Yes," Sam agreed. "I'll put the badger away." As the picture rolled up and the metal rod returned to the arm of his wheelchair, he asked: "So, what does SPOT stand for?"

Chapter 10

Mr Trenchard joined Class 3D on the flat roof over the science block.

"What does the satellite look like?" Alfie asked.

"What satellite?" Mr Trenchard asked. Five minutes later, after consulting his paperwork, he told them: "It's a metal ball, about this big." He pointed to Harry's head. "Only without a face on it," he added, in case there was any confusion. "Or ears. Or hair, actually."

"Got it!"

Alice said.

She pointed out
where she had seen it
through her binoculars.
Everyone else raised their
binoculars and turned to look.

"Yes, that's the fellow," Mr

Trenchard confirmed. "You see – no ears at all. So what now? How will you retrieve the satellite?"

"Badgers," Harry said.

"I think we've moved on from that," Alfie told him.

"I've designed this," Beth said, and unrolled a complicated plan she had drawn. It showed Sam sitting in his wheelchair. From the front, two long grabber arms were extended. Details showed how the arms were jointed and what motors and controls were needed to make them reach over the fence, pick up the satellite and lift it back over.

"Oh, this is marvellous," Mr Trenchard said, examining the plan. "Very impressive. And I'm an expert you know," he went on.

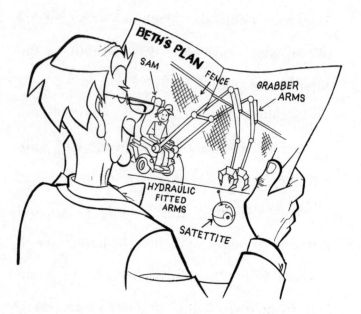

"Oh yes, I used to design secret weapons that could be hidden in fields – at the Department of Advanced Field Technology. It's better known by its initials, of course."

"That's DAFT," Alfie said.

"Completely bonkers," Trenchard agreed, "but it kept us busy. Right then, over to you."

Beth found all the equipment she needed in the science block, and with help from the rest of Class 3D she set about welding and bolting and fixing wide steel arms and enormous motors to the front of Sam's wheelchair.

"I'm not sure this will work," Alfie said when they'd finished.

"Just because it wasn't your idea," said. Chloe.

"Nonsense, it's perfect," said Beth. She let go of the metal claw she had just attached to the end of one of the long arms and stepped back.

Slowly, Sam's wheelchair pitched forwards and he fell out. "Bit too heavy," he said.

"Go on a diet," Chloe advised.

"Not me – Beth's metal arms."

Harry looked stunned. "Beth has metal arms?"

"We just need to hang on the back of the chair and balance it," said Alice.

With the rest of Class 3D hanging on the back and the metal arms sticking out and up from the front, Sam's wheelchair moved very slowly even at full speed.

"You'll burn my motors out," he complained.

"Sam's got motors?"

"Be quiet, Harry," Jack said. "You know he has."

"There, you see," said Beth as they continued to roll forwards. "I told you this would work."

Then the wheelchair reached the door. Usually it fit through easily. But not now. One metal arm collided with the wall on one side

of the doorway. The other one tangled in the

handle of the open door. The sudden jolt

knocked everyone off the back of the chair

and it toppled forwards into the doorway, the two new metal arms twisting off and landing in a shattered heap on either side.

"That was Alfie's fault," Chloe said. A bit unfairly, Alfie thought.

"So what do we do now?" Alice asked. "Those SPUD agents won't be fooled by the fake crash site for long."

"I think," said Alfie, "that we should play a game of football."

After some discussion about who should go in goal, Alfie managed to explain why he *really* wanted to play football.

Chloe shook her head and folded her arms. "Wasting more time," she said. "I saw three SPUD agents heading for Mrs Prendergast's just now."

"Let's hope they're on their tea break," said Beth.

"I don't think they are," Jack told them. "They're searching the garden – you can see them through the fence, look."

Everyone agreed they'd better start playing football at once. Sam had just about recovered from his ordeal with the metal arms, but even so he said he'd sit the game out rather than whiz round and knock the ball about.

"Just as well," Alice told Alfie. "He's lethal in that thing. Doesn't just go for the ball. Sent Harry flying last time we played. Scooped him up on the foot rests and then couldn't see where he was going. They both disappeared out of the grounds and Sergeant Custer had to go after them in the school Armoured Personnel Carrier."

"I think that as we couldn't arrange my badger plan, I should be the one to do it," Jack said.

Alfie shrugged. "Fine by me. You know what to say?"

Jack nodded.

"Let's play for a few minutes first," Alfie said, "just so it doesn't look suspicious."

"Not too long," Chloe warned.

After five minutes, they all agreed it was time. Jack took a tremendous run-up and gave the ball a colossal kick. It flew high up in the air.

"Oh, my goodness," Jack announced loudly. "Well, will you look at that. Sorry, looks like it's going over."

"Oh, Jack!" everyone said as the ball flew over the fence and into Mrs Prendergast's garden. SPUD agents dived for cover and hid in the shrubbery.

"I suppose," Jack said loudly, "that I'd better go and ask if I can get it back." He winked, and ran off towards the main school gates.

Everyone waited expectantly. Soon Jack ran back triumphantly. He was holding a round object about the size of Harry's head but with no ears. "I got it!" he exclaimed. "The ball landed right next to the satellite. What luck!"

They all stared at what Jack was holding. "That's our football," Alfie said.

"Well, yes. I kicked it over the fence and went

to get it back, remember. But it worked, Alfie – now we know exactly where the satellite is. All we need to do is find and train some badgers."

"Er," Beth said, "I don't think that was quite what Alfie had in mind. Was it, Alfie?"

"Then he should have explained better," Chloe said. "Now the SPUD agents will get the satellite and it's Alfie's fault. Look – they're searching that part of the garden now."

Alfie could see several men in dark glasses approaching where Jack had found the satellite. He quickly took the ball from Jack and kicked it high over the fence. "My turn," he said.

A few minutes later, having asked Mrs Prendergast politely if he could get his ball back, apologised for kicking it over *again* and promised that yes, they would play further away from her fence, Alfie was in the garden. He could see the satellite nestling under a holly bush at the edge of a flowerbed. The football was close by. But so was a SPUD agent, searching on hands and knees for the satellite...

The man drew back into cover as Alfie approached. Alfie reached the football and kicked it towards the bushes, running quickly after it...

Soon, Alfie was back with his friends from Class 3D. He was carrying a silver ball about the size of Harry's head. Lights flashed round the edge, and it made bleep- bleep noises.

"That," Harry said seriously, "is *not* our football."

There was a special assembly before the end of school, where Mr Trenchard thanked Class 3D for their excellent work recovering the whatever-it-was. He gave Miss Jones a certificate that had been specially printed by Mr Cryption. It said:

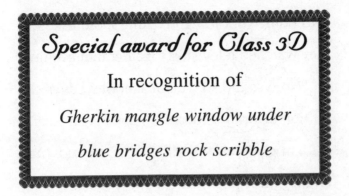

Special award for Class 3D

In recognition of

Gherkin mangle window under

blue bridges rock scribble

Everyone was delighted. Even Chloe spared Alfie a smile. But then she seemed to realise what she was doing, and it changed into a frown.

"And I gather from someone's father..." Mr Trenchard said, pausing to wink knowingly at Harry, "... that the SPUD agents sent to find the satellite, thought they'd worked out where it crashed and have returned to SPUD HQ with a football. They are, even as I speak, trying to find out how it works."

"I think you just kick it," Harry said.

"No homework tonight?" Alfie's dad asked as they watched television together that evening.

"No. We did so well at school we were let off homework for today."

"I'm glad you're settling in," Dad said. "You know, I wasn't really sure if you'd like it."

"Dad, can I ask you something?"

"Of course you can, Alfie. Something about school?"

"Sort of. Dad – are you *really* a postman?" Alfie asked.

Alfie's dad smiled and nodded. But he said nothing.

Agent Alfie will return in
On Her Majesty's Postal Service.

Hedgehog Slab Illusion

Huh?

Well, Mr Cryption might seem to be talking rubbish, but in fact everything he says is in code. Here are some of the code words that Mr Cryption uses together with what they really mean – provided by the Government Rapid Analysis Decoding and Encryption Section (GRADES). Other words have not yet been deciphered – perhaps you can work them out?

You can also use the list to say things in code, like Mr Cryption. But be warned – if you do, no one will know what you are talking about!

Codeword	Meaning
Alert	Letter
Antelopes	Satellite
Anthology	Collection
Artichoke	Watch out
Bananas	Tummy
Bath	Big tub of water

Codeword	Meaning
Binoculars	Colour
Blue	Difficult
Bridges	Dangerous
Butter	Damaged
Cardigans	Success
Carpet	Unexpected
Casement	Enclosed frame
Cashflow	Expensive
Crisis	Envelope
Dilemma	If
Doom	Clever
Enormous	Worked
Extraction	Code-breaking
Fester	No
Flammable	When
Flippers	Flippers
Frosting	Frosting
Garden	Talking
Geography	Need
Gherkin	Outstanding

Codeword	Meaning
Gold	Stay
Golf	Camouflage
Hamster	Teacher
Hat stand	Saucepan
Heart-shaped	Secret
Hedgehog	Quick
Igloo	Completely
Imposter	Blanket
Identity	In
Illusion	Code
Luggage	Responsibility
Mangle	Achievement
Marbles	Brains
Nightmare	Hoorah!
Office	Not good
Pest	Hiding
Phoenix	Again
Pig	Today
Quibble	Better
Rewind	Recover

Codeword	Meaning
Rock	Circumstances
Safety	Pink
Scribble	Message Ends
Shakespeare	Muddled
Slab	Guide
Sleepwalker	Deception
Slingshot	Hurt
Submarine	After school
Tailor	Lessons
Under	Extremely
Vikings	Fake
Violin	Stringed musical instrument
Visible	Detention
Window	Under
Wobble	Badly
Xylophonics	Good morning
Zebra	Black and white striped animal like a horse
Zero	Netting